Chinese Bedtime Stories

By Tina Chen

Contents

1. The Praying Mantis and the Cicada

A long time ago in ancient China, there was a philosopher named Zhuangzi.

One day, he took a walk in a large, grassy field. Suddenly, there was a great rush of wind and a big, mysterious bird alighted on a tree in the nearby orchard. Zhuangzi followed the bird into the orchard and pulled out his slingshot as he crept closer. Because of his curiosity, he desperately wanted to get a better look at the bird. As he approached the tree, he saw that the bird was intently watching a praying mantis hiding in the tall grass. So intent on its prey, the bird did not notice Zhuangzi. Then, turning his gaze to the praying mantis, Zhuangzi realized that the praying mantis was not aware of the bird because it was too busy attempting to catch a nearby cicada. Zhuangzi set down his sling shot and observed the scene in front of him, deep in thought.

"These animals are so focused on the prey in front of them that they are not even aware of the danger behind them." Zhuangzi reflected. He was a philosopher, after all.

"What do you think you're doing in my orchard, thief? Stealing my fruit, are you?" A voice behind him shouted suddenly, jolting Zhuangzi out of his thoughts. Zhuangzi spun around to find the owner of the orchard stomping toward him.

"I am so sorry, sir. I was only watching that bird over there. I did not steal any fruit," Zhuangzi said as he pointed at the mystery bird.

"I don't want your excuses. I saw you messing around the fruit tree. Just get out of here, and don't come to my orchard again," the owner snarled.

"Yes, sir." Zhuangzi bowed and left, the owner watching him the whole way out.

It had been a few days since Zhuangzi had been in the orchard, but the incident was still bothering him. Finally, one of his favorite students asked him, "What is wrong?"

Zhuangzi sighed and set down the scroll he had been reading. "I was in the orchard the other day watching a bird watch a praying mantis watch a cicada, each so intent on the next that it didn't realize what great danger lurked behind it. I was impressed by how ignorant they were, and even stated it out loud, yet I myself was oblivious to the fact that I was being watched too."

2. The Secret of the Special Scale

In ancient China, there were two shops that both sold rice. They were right across the street from each other and competed for the same customers.

One day, the owner of one of the rice shops came up with a new tactic. He ordered the scale maker to make a scale that made one pound equivalent to 15 ounces, even though one pound is truly equal to 16 ounces. With this incorrect scale, the owner would be able to cheat customers out of an ounce of rice. Then, the owner paid the man a fair sum of money to keep quiet about the scale. As the owner was talking to the scale maker, the owner's daughter-in-law happened to walk past, and she overheard her father-in-law planning the new scale. An idea came to her and she slipped into the room to talk to the scale maker once her father-in-law left.

"I apologize--- my father is a bit absentminded. When he told you to make a scale with 15 ounces equivalent to a pound, he actually meant 17 ounces. Please make the scale show that 17 ounces equal a pound instead," the daughter-in-law lied. She knew that cheating would never win over customers.

"He did not seem absentminded or distracted to me. In fact, he warned me to keep quiet about this," the scale maker replied suspiciously.

"Oh, no. He has already told us about his plan for the scale this morning, but has been distracted all day, since he has a meeting with the governor. He is worried about it, especially since the governor buys from the other shop," the daughter-in-law claimed.

All of this was, of course, not true. The daughter-in-law smiled convincingly. Even more convincing was the pouch of coins that dangled from her hand. The scale maker sighed and took the coins.

A year had passed and the rice shop prospered. Nearly all the customers went to the rice shop with the special scale because they soon realized that one pound of rice from that store lasted longer. Now it was Chinese New Year and the owner of the rice shop was holding his annual party.

"My dear friends and family, I have a secret that I have yet to tell you. This secret has made our shop prosper. Our store has a special scale. A while ago, I had the scale maker create a scale that sets 15 ounces equal to one pound," the owner announced. The room was silent and everyone stared at the owner, shocked. Then, the owner's daughter-in-law got up and kneeled in front of her father-in-law.

"I am truly sorry, Father. I did not tell you, for I feared that you would be angry. After you talked to the scale maker, I went into his workshop and told him to make 17 ounces equal one pound," the daughter-in-law admitted. The shop owner was quiet. Then he abruptly stood up and left the party.

The next day, the owner handed control of the shop to his daughter-in-law. He knew that with her business sense, the rice shop would prosper for years to come.

3. Keeping Calm

During the Song Dynasty, there lived a boy called Sima Guang, who loved to play hide and seek with his friends. One time, they decided to play on the side of the mountain that was near their village. As they ran to hide, one of the boys ran downhill, tripped on a stone, and fell into the gigantic barrel full of water. The boy cried out, floundering in the deep water. The game stopped and his friends ran away, yelling, "Help! Help! Help!" Only one boy remained: Sima Guang.

He stayed behind, knowing that by the time the other boys returned with help, his friend would already be dead, for the boy could not swim. Sima Guang looked around, searching for a way to save his friend, but found nothing. Desperately, Sima Guang wrapped his hands around one of the planks of the barrel and pulled with all his might. He pulled and pulled and pulled, until suddenly, the plank gave way and bent out of place. Water poured out onto the ground, seeping out of the bucket. By the time help arrived, Sima Guang had already saved his friend from drowning.

Years later, Sima Guang became a well-respected prime minister of the Song Dynasty.

4. Home, Sweet Home

Once upon a time, during a period of war, there was a young boy named Mengzi, who lived with his mother. They were poor, and there was not enough money to send Mengzi, the son, to school.

They lived by the cemetery where the land and housing was cheap because no one wanted to live near the graves. Everyday, mourners, who were people hired to cry at funerals, passed by their house, weeping, as they made their way to the cemetery. When he was bored, Mengzi would shadow the mourners and cry with them. His mother, however, wanted her son to be more than a hired mourner.

So they moved and settled by a meat market, Mengzi quickly adapted to his new environment. The very next day, he set up his own stall and joined the shouting, noisy butchers, although he had nothing to sell. Again, his mother was exasperated, especially after Mengzi declared that he wanted to be a butcher when he grew up. Seeing no other choice, his mother packed up their things, and they moved yet again.

This time, their new home was right next to a school. Like all his other homes, Mengzi found his new surroundings exciting. He hid beneath the windows of the school and listened in on classes. Everyday, he learned more and more. Finally, his mother felt satisfied. She knew her son was getting educated.

When he grew up, Mengzi became a famous philosopher. He was the second most famous philosopher in the history of China after Confucius.

5. Rain or Shine

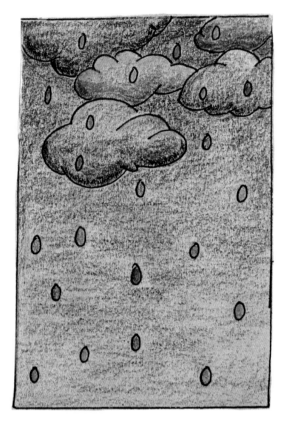

Once, in ancient China, there lived a woman who had two daughters, both of whom were married. The elder daughter's husband sold umbrellas. The younger daughter's husband made noodles. On sunny days, no one bought the umbrellas, and on rainy days, it was impossible to make noodles because the noodles had to be sun dried. So every day, the woman cried, whether it was a rainy day or a sunny day. On rainy days, she cried for her younger daughter, and on sunny days, she cried for her older daughter. She always worried about her son-in-laws' jobs.

One day, while she was crying, a wise, old woman walked by.

"Why are you crying on such a bright, sunny day?" The wise woman asked.

"My older daughter is married to an umbrella merchant. Today the sun is shining, so no one will buy an umbrella," the woman responded through her tears.

"Ah. Then you will be happy tomorrow. From looking at the clouds, I can tell it will rain tomorrow, and people will buy umbrellas again," the older woman said.

"Rain? Tomorrow? Oh, no!" The woman cried. The old woman blinked in surprise.

"I thought you wanted rain, so it could bring good business for your son-in-law."

"Yes, but my younger daughter's husband makes noodles, and without the sun, the noodles will not dry properly. Oh, no!" The woman repeated. The old woman raised an eyebrow.

"Think of it this way; on sunny days, your younger daughter will be able to make noodles, and on rainy days, your older daughter will sell many umbrellas," the old woman explained. The mother paused, tears stopping.

"Oh. I had never thought of it that way," the woman said.

"Now, you will have a reason to be happy everyday," the old woman laughed.

From then on, the woman never cried. Instead, she smiled all the time. On rainy days, she was happy for her older daughter and on sunny days, she was happy for her younger daughter.

6. Two Brothers

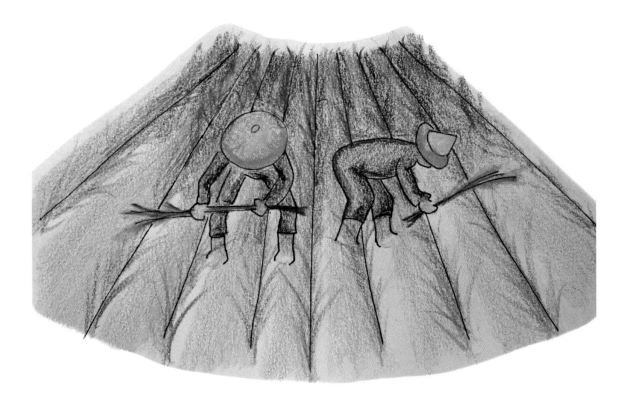

A long, long time ago, in Ancient China, there lived two brothers who worked the fields together. The older brother was married and had children, while the younger brother had yet to marry. They planted and tended the land together, and when it came time to harvest the rice, they harvested together. Then, one night, the older brother thought, "My younger brother needs money to get married. If he has more rice, he can sell it and finally marry." So that night, in the dark, the older brother separated a portion of his rice and dumped it into his brother's bag.

Meanwhile, the younger brother was thinking, "My brother is married and has children. He needs to feed his family." He, too, took some of his own rice and secretly added it to his brother's portion of rice. Neither of them mentioned giving rice to the other, afraid that the extra rice would be refused out of politeness.

For a while, the two brothers continued to give each other rice at night. Soon, they realized that even though they were giving away rice, their supply of rice never dwindled. One night, they ran into each other as they carried their rice to the other's house. Laughing, they hugged each other.

7. Sai Wong and his Horse

On the outskirts of a small village during the Han Dynasty, an old man called Sai Wong lived with his son on their farm. One sunny day, their horse escaped, galloping across the fields and disappearing into the surrounding forest before the son had time to catch it.

That day, the son searched the fields and forest for the white horse, but found nothing. Finally, after the sun set, he returned home, tired and disappointed. Over dinner, he sadly told his father about the lost horse. At that time, horses were very expensive because they were the fastest means of transportation. His father, however, was unperturbed. Patting his son's shoulder, Sai Wong declared, "Don't worry. Perhaps the loss of that horse will actually bring us good luck." His son was shocked, but he nodded quietly, too tired to argue with his father.

One morning a few months later, the son woke up to find the white horse waiting outside their farm with a wild, black horse beside it. He was thrilled and rushed to lead the two horses to the stables.

But when he eagerly told his father about the new horse, Sai Wong merely smiled and warned his son, "Who knows? While this new horse may seem lucky, it might lead to bad luck." His son looked doubtful, but he just shrugged and cheerfully left to tend to the new horse.

That week, as the son was riding the newly trained horse, one of the herding dogs on the farm accidentally scared the horse, making him buck off the son. He flew through the air, landing painfully on the hard ground. His father found him clutching his right leg, and with his father's help, the son limped into the house. One of their neighbors sprinted to find the village doctor.

As Sai Wong and his son waited for the doctor to arrive, Sai Wong gently patted his son's arm. "Don't be so worried. Perhaps, this is actually good luck in disguise," Sai Wong comforted. His son stared at him in disbelief.

The next week, the Xiongnu, a group of invaders, reached their kingdom, so all the young men from their village were called to join the army. Months later, when the war was over, none of the men from their village returned. All had died on the battlefield, except Sai Wong's son who had to stay behind because of his broken leg. His father's words had been right once again.

8. Two-headed Snake

A long time ago, a boy named Sunshu Ao lived with his mother. One day, as he walked from the marketplace back to their house, he happened upon a two-headed snake. When he got home, his mother gently asked him why he looked so upset.

"I saw a two-headed snake on the way home," Sunshu Ao cried. "It was terrifying!"

His mother rubbed his back comfortingly and asked, "Well, where is the snake now?"

"I heard that whoever sees a two-headed snake will die, so I killed it and buried. That way, no one else will see it and die," Sunshu Ao explained. "I know I will die, though, since I saw it."

His mother reassured him, "You saved many other people. What you did is a good thing, and good deeds always bring good luck."

As it turned out, Sunshu Ao did not die from seeing the snake. In fact, he later became the prime minister of Chu.

9. A Rooster's Egg

One day during the Warring States era, the emperor devised a plan to get one of his advisors fired. His advisor's name was Gan Mao, and the emperor issued Gan Mao an order: he must find three eggs laid by a rooster in three days' time. Gan Mao went home and paced back and forth. Where on earth could he find eggs laid by a rooster? They did not exist. His twelve-year-old grandson Gan Luo asked him what was wrong, and upon learning of the emperor's command, Gan Luo told his grandfather, "Tomorrow, let me go to the emperor. I have a plan."

The next day, Gan Luo set off for the emperor's palace in his grandfather's place. When the emperor saw him, he did not recognize Gan Luo, and asked, "Who are you? I do not recognize you."

Gan Luo bowed and said, "I am Gan Luo, grandson of Gan Mao."

"Ah, I see," the emperor said. "And why is Gan Mao not here?"

"My grandfather is at home giving birth to his child, so he could not make it to work today," Gan Luo replied very calmly.

"Ridiculous!" The emperor exclaimed. "That is impossible— men cannot give birth!"

"And if men cannot give birth, then how can roosters lay eggs?" Gan Luo asked fearlessly. Gan Luo's calm answer surprised the emperor, and helped him understand the ridiculousness of rooster's eggs.

The emperor was so impressed by Gan Luo's intelligence that he never bothered his grandfather again, and even made Gan Luo a minister.

10. Bandits and the Blackberry Tree

During the Han Dynasty, China was made up of many small kingdoms. In one of the smaller kingdoms, chaos reigned, and there was no law or order. Many people became bandits or thieves because it was impossible to survive otherwise.

In this kingdom, there was a boy named Cai Shun. His father had passed away, and daily life was tough for him and his mother. Cai Shun was very devoted to his mother, and every day he tried to come up with new ways to get food for the two of them. This was an extremely hard task since food had become scarce.

One day, Cai Shun was walking along a path in the woods when he spotted a blackberry tree. Excited, he climbed up the tree and picked as many blackberries as he could, filling up two baskets. Suddenly, a group of bandits appeared, spotted his baskets of blackberries, and snatched them from Cai Shun. As the bandits were about to leave, the leader noticed something odd.

"Why is one basket full of ripe blackberries and the other full of sour, unripe berries?" the bandit asked curiously.

"The ripe ones are for my mother, because they are sweet," Cai Shun explained. "The small or unripe ones are for me."

The bandits were moved by Cai Shun's filial piety, respect, and devotion to his mother. They not only returned the baskets of blackberries to Cai Shun, but also gifted him with three baskets of rice.

11. To Weigh an Elephant

Once upon a time, Emperor Cao Cao received an elephant as a gift. Cao Cao wanted to know how heavy the elephant was, but nobody could come up with a way to weigh the elephant. After all, the elephant would never fit on a normal scale. Then, Cao Cao's six-year-old son Cao Chong thought of a solution.

"I have a way," Cao Chong announced. He led the elephant onto a boat floating in the river. Next, using a knife, Cao Chong made a small mark on the side of the boat at the waterline, which is the height that the water reaches on the boat. Next, he led the elephant back onto shore and ordered Cao Cao's men to move rock after rock onto the boat until the river water reached the mark he had made earlier with the knife.

"Now," Cao Chong said, "if we measure the weight of all the rocks on the ship, we will know the weight of the elephant."

For his cleverness, Cao Chong received praise from the Emperor's advisors.

Chinese Bedtime Stories

2018 By Tina Chen

Made in the USA
Coppell, TX
02 January 2020